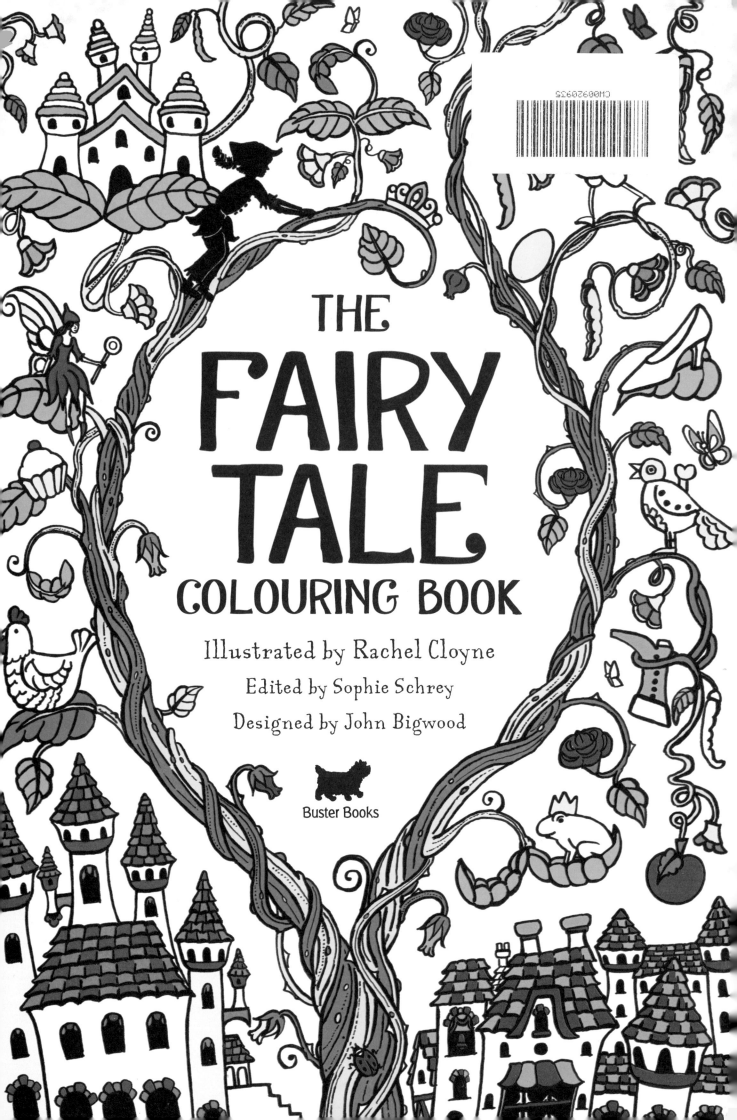

THE FAIRY TALE COLOURING BOOK

Illustrated by Rachel Cloyne

Edited by Sophie Schrey

Designed by John Bigwood

Buster Books

These fairy tale
pictures were coloured
and completed by:

.....Lyla Roe....Level♡Piano

Look out for the fairy on every page.

As Little Red Riding Hood entered the woods, she was met by a wolf.

The Little Mermaid
loved everything about
the world above.

Rapunzel, Rapunzel, let down your golden hair ...

The Queen put a hard pea under the mattresses to test if she was a true princess.

Jack climbed up the beanstalk.

The Snow Queen lived in the far north, only coming south to bring the cold weather with her.

She will sleep until a prince comes to awaken her with a kiss ...

The sound of a pipe wafted through the streets of Hamelin.

Cinderella, you must leave the
ball by midnight ...

Mirror, mirror, on the wall ...

The Emperor was sent a beautiful clockwork nightingale.

The princes rowed the twelve princesses across the lake.

The prince said he would marry the girl whose foot fit the glass slipper.

The carpenter named the puppet Pinocchio.

The dwarves loved having
Snow White in their cottage.

Hansel and Gretel found a house made of sweets.

The frog would turn into a handsome prince.

Shoemaker

When the shoemaker went to bed, two little elves set to work making shoes ...

The wicked queen turned the eleven princes into swans.

The Little Mermaid watched the prince from the water.

First published in Great Britain in 2014 by Buster Books, an imprint of Michael O'Mara Books Limited, 9 Lion Yard, Tremadoc Road, London SW4 7NQ
Copyright © Buster Books 2014
Illustrations copyright © Rachel Cloyne 2014
ISBN: 978-1-78055-252-1
6 8 10 9 7
This book was printed in January 2017 by Shenzhen Wing King Tong Paper Products Co. Ltd., Shenzhen, Guangdong, China.

 www.busterbooks.co.uk  Buster Children's Books   @BusterBooks